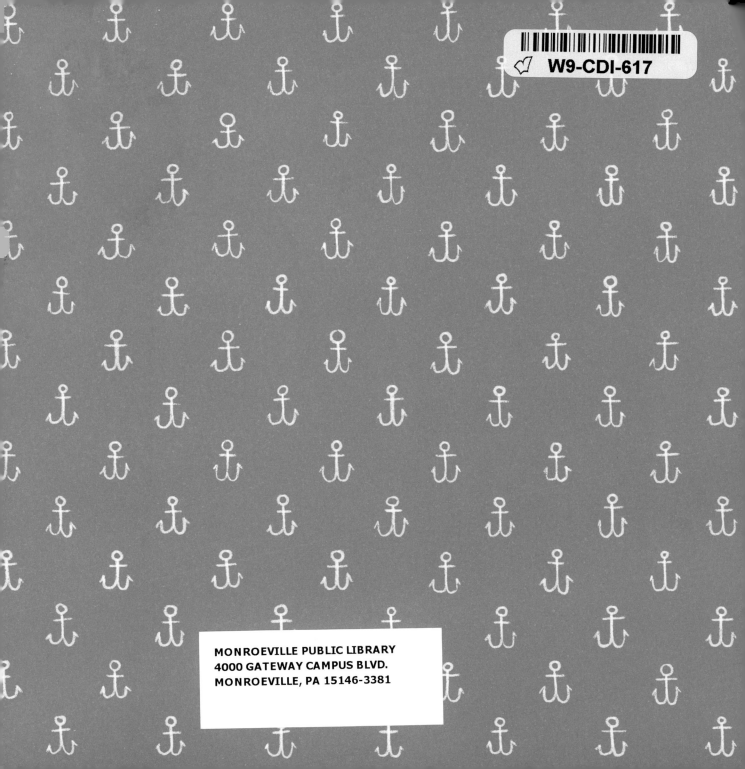

Where does a PIRATE go Potty?

Written by Dawn Babb Prochovnic

Illustrated by Jacob Souva

WEST
MARGIN
PRESS

For Nikko, whose antics inspired this story, many moons ago. –D.P.

For Austin and Lucas, two of my favorite buccaneers. –J.S.

Library of Congress Control Number: 2019905566

ISBN 9781513262406 (hardbound)
ISBN 9781513262413 (e-book)

Printed in China
22 21 20 19 1 2 3 4 5

Published by West Margin Press®

WEST
MARGIN
PRESS

WestMarginPress.com

Proudly distributed by Ingram Publisher Services

WEST MARGIN PRESS
Publishing Director: Jennifer Newens
Marketing Manager: Angela Zbornik
Editor: Olivia Ngai
Design & Production: Rachel Lopez Metzger

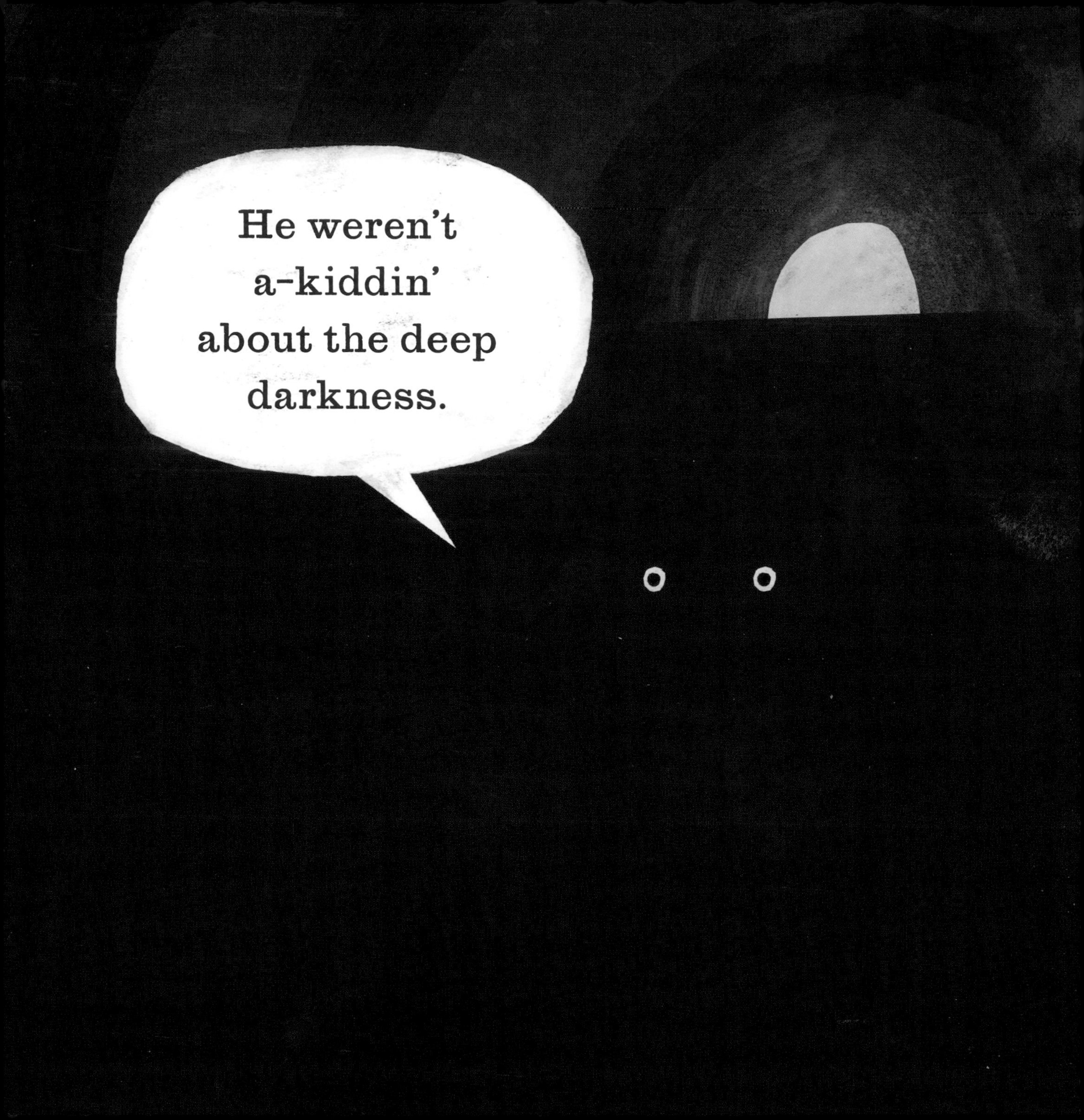
He weren't a-kiddin' about the deep darkness.

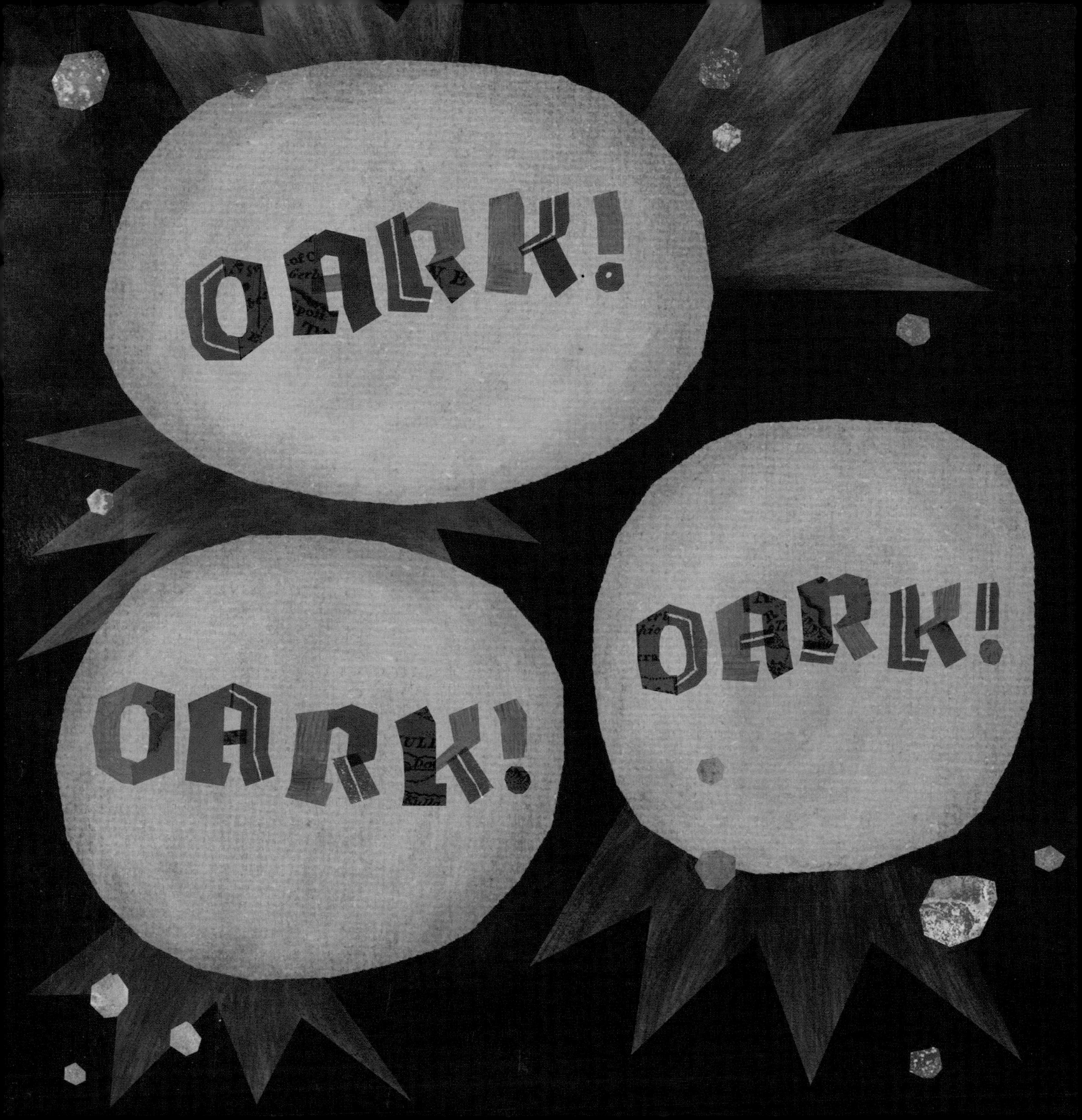
OARK!
OARK!
OARK!

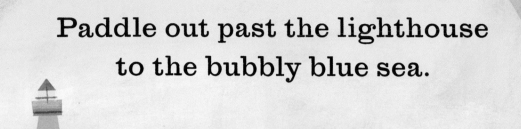

Paddle out past the lighthouse
to the bubbly blue sea.

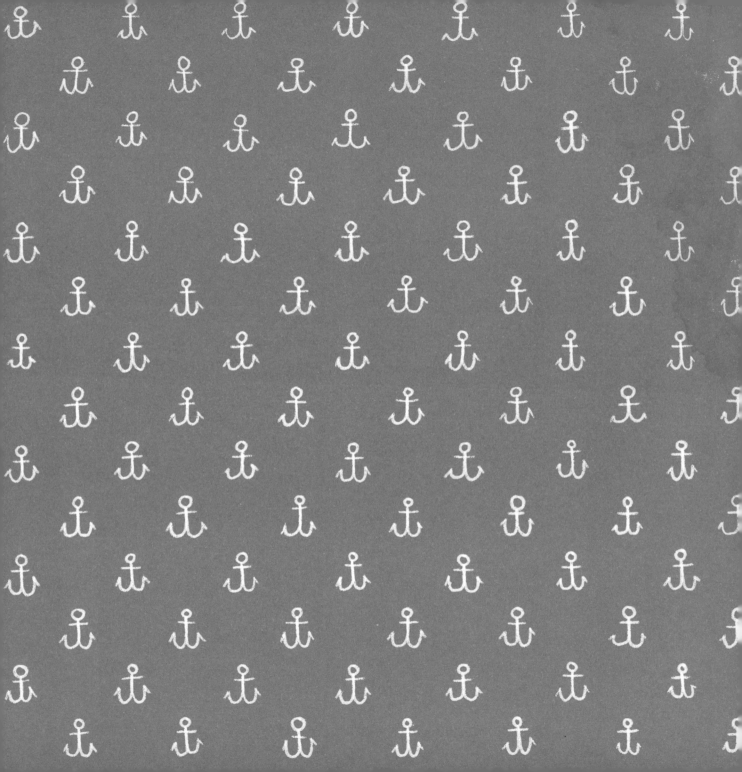